CatKid

Three's a crowd

Hi! My name is CatKid.

That means I'm one whole-half cat and one whole-half kid. It also means I'm two full halves cute! Most people have never seen a half-cat, half-kid before. Know why? Because I'm special, that's why!

CatKid

Three's a Crowd

Brian James

illustrated by
Ned Woodman

SCHOLASTIC INC.

New York Toronto London Auckland Sydney
Mexico City New Delhi Hong Kong Buenos Aires

ISBN-13: 978-0-439-88857-8
ISBN-10: 0-439-88857-3

Book design by Tim Hall

12 11 10 9 8 7 6 5 4 3 2 1   8 9 10 11 12 13/0
40
Printed in the U.S.A.
First printing, February 2008

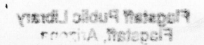

Chapter 1

A Yippy Skippy Morning!

I, CatKid, race off the bus when it pulls into my school. That's because morning recess starts the second I step onto the playground. And I just LOVE that recess stuff! If I were in charge of spelling things, I would spell recess F-U-N!

"'Bye, Mrs. Bus Driver!" I shout on my way out. That's called being polite, and my mom says I should always be polite.

My bus driver says good-bye right back. She's one polite lady, too!

"Come on, let's go," I say to my best friend, Maddie.

Then I grab Maddie's hand and hurry with her to the monkey bars. The monkey bars are my favorite place on the entire playground.

"Hey CatKid," Maddie says, "let's race to the top!"

"You bet," I say. "On your mark, get set, GO!" Then I start running as fast as I can. My cat half is extra fast, then I leap right to the top!

"I win!" I say. Then I smile my whiskers real proud. I like that winning stuff.

Maddie stops running when she sees me. She's too giggly to run. She always gets giggly when I leap to the top of the monkey bars.

"That was *cat*-tastic!" Maddie says. Then she claps her hands. "I thought you might win, so I brought this," she says. She reaches into her backpack and takes out a

yummy chocolate chip cookie. "It's your first-place prize!"

"It's the best prize ever!" I shout as I scramble down from the monkey bars. I take that cookie and I gobble it up in one bite.

Maddie gets giggly all over again. She thinks that gobbling stuff is funny stuff.

"I've got something for you, too," I say. I reach into my backpack and pull out a piece of paper. "Ta-da!" I say and hand the paper to Maddie. It's a drawing of two goldfish.

"These are our goldfish!" Maddie says.

I nod. Mrs. Sparrow gave them to us as first prize for winning a treasure hunt at the aquarium. Now those fish are our pets. They live at Maddie's house and they're best friends, like us.

"Thanks! I'm going to hang it up in my room," Maddie says.

"You're welcome," I say. That's called being a good friend.

Next, Maddie and I decide to play a hand-clapping game.

"Ready?" Maddie asks.

"Ready spaghetti!" I say.

Then we start chanting "Miss Mary Mack." Only know what? We changed the words, that's what! Instead of "Miss Mary Mack," we chant "Miss Special

4

Cat." It's our secret version that only we know.

"I am half-cat, cat, cat . . .
Sitting on a mat, mat, mat . . .
With a stripy tail, tail, tail . . .
And a fish-shaped hat, hat, hat . . ."

We don't get very far because just as we sing that "hat, hat, hat" part, we see our friends Kendra and Lauren running toward the monkey  bars. They are in Mrs. Sparrow's second-grade class, too.

"It looks like they're racing," Maddie says.

"Yeah," I say. Then I lick my lips. "I wonder if that means they have cookies." I, CatKid, just love those cookies! I like them almost as much as fish, and fish is what I call the yummiest food ever invented.

"Silly kitty," Maddie says and giggles again.

I giggle too because "silly kitty" is one funny pet name.

"Hey," Kendra says.

"Hey right back," I say.

I'm just about to ask them if they were racing when Lauren says they have a surprise.

"Yippy skippy, I love a surprise!" I shout. Then I cross my fingers and hope the surprise is a cookie. Cookies are a great surprise. "Is it a cookie?" I ask.

"Nope," Lauren says.

I make a frowny face and cross my arms. I'm not so sure I'm going to like that surprise if it's not a cookie.

"It's better than that," Kendra says.

That makes me scratch my head. I can't even think of a better surprise. "What is it?" I ask.

"Our class is getting a new student!" Kendra yells.

Me and Maddie clap our hands, only not like in the game. This time, we clap our hands because we're so excited.

"WOWWIE!" I shout.

"Double wowwie!" Maddie shouts.

"I hope it's not a boy," Lauren says.

"Me too," Kendra says.

My eyes go all big. I don't even want to think about that. "Me, three," I say. Then I hold my nose and stick out my tongue. "Boys are stinky," I say. "Except Preston!"

I add, because Preston is my friend even if he is a boy.

Just then, the bell rings.

That bell means it's the end of morning recess.

Then we all start running to our classroom. But it's not a race. We're too excited about the new student to think about racing.

Chapter 2

The Best Welcome Party Ever!

My whole class is whispering about the new student. That's because Mrs. Sparrow says the new student is going to join our class soon. I can't even wait to meet that new student!

We all have our hands raised up in the air. That's because we all have questions about the new student.

My question is the most important question.

So I raise my hand up extra high and wave my tail around. Then I stand up and hop around. Mrs. Sparrow must be

able to tell that my question is important because she calls on me first.

"Yes, CatKid," she says.

"Um . . . Mrs. Sparrow?" I ask. "Is this new student a boy student or a girl student?"

All the other hands go down.

That was the same thing they all wanted to ask. I just knew that boy or girl question was important!

"We should welcome our new classmate just the same either way," Mrs. Sparrow says. That makes my whole class moan and groan because that answer is a tricky answer.

"I know it's a boy," Billy says.

I spin my tail right around. "How do you know?" I ask.

"Because!" Billy says. "There are already more girls than boys in our class. So it's only fair."

That's a true fact. There are exactly four more girls in my class than boys. That's not even counting Mrs. Sparrow because she's a grown-up.

"I don't care if it's a boy or a girl as long it's not *half*-anything," Shelly says to me. That's because she's snotty and doesn't like my cat half. Plus, she's my number one un-best friend. "Half anything is weird," she says.

"Yeah, well, you're half meanie, so there!" I say right back.

Then I cover my mouth real quick because Mrs. Sparrow doesn't like name-calling. She gives both of us a frowny look. But it's not even my fault. I have to stick up for my cat half. It's one of my favorite halves.

Mrs. Sparrow tells us that we need to practice saying, "Welcome to our class!" She wants us all to say it at the same time and to use our outdoor voices so that we're extra loud. She says that will make our classmate feel super welcome.

I, CatKid, love using my outdoor voice inside! So when it's time to practice, I holler out the loudest. Only guess what? I holler so loud that it makes Maddie giggle. That's why we have to practice a few times until we get it perfect, because perfect means absolutely no giggling!

Just then, there's a knock on our class-room door!

We all go quiet as Mrs. Sparrow walks over to the door and peeks out. Then she smiles real wide.

"Class, I want you to give Kristie a big welcome," she says as she pulls the door wide open.

And guess what?

A girl walks into our class-room, that's what!

"YIPPY!" I shout. "I told you it would be a girl," I whisper to Billy.

Then our entire class shouts, "WELCOME TO OUR CLASS!" just like we practiced.

Kristie doesn't shout anything, but she waves.

"She looks shy," Kendra whispers.

"She's probably just afraid of CatKid," Shelly whispers.

"Maybe she's afraid of your face," I growl.

"Okay class, settle down," Mrs. Sparrow says. Settle down is a nice teacher way to tell us to zip our mouths closed.

After everyone is quiet, Mrs. Sparrow says she is going to pick one of us to show Kristie around. She asks if there are any volunteers.

All the girls in my class raise their hands.

Bradley raises his hand, too. That's because he's a know-it-all. Plus, he's a show-off. "Since I know everything the best, I should be the one to show Kristie around," he says.

I roll my eyes and make a huff. Sometimes that Bradley really gets on my cat nerves.

I'm glad when Mrs. Sparrow doesn't pick him.

I'm double glad when she does pick Maddie.

"Maddie, would you like to be Kristie's buddy for today?" Mrs. Sparrow asks. Maddie nods her head up and down and down and up!

I smile my whiskers real wide because Maddie is one good buddy. Plus, it means I get to help show Kristie around, too.

Because me and Maddie are best friends, and that's what best friends do. They share.

We are going to be the best welcome party there ever was!

Chapter 3

The Trouble With Sharing

After we say the Pledge, Mrs. Sparrow tells the class to go over to the story-time rug.

That's my favorite place in the whole classroom! So I grab my tail and spin around on one foot. That's what I, CatKid, call my happy dance.

I rush over to Maddie. She likes it when I do my happy dance. It makes her all giggly.

Only know what?

This time she doesn't get giggly, that's what! That's because she's busy telling

Kristie all about the story-time rug and doesn't see my happy dance. I don't mind, though, because part of her buddy job is telling Kristie those things.

"Mrs. Sparrow reads us a story here every day," Maddie explains. "All kinds of stories. Stories about unicorns are my favorite."

"My favorite stories are the ones about dogs," Kristie says.

My ears perk right up.

Then I make a growly face and cross my arms.

"I, CatKid, do NOT like dogs! Not even a tiny bit," I tell Kristie. "Stories about cats are better."

"Who's that?" Kristie whispers to Maddie.

"I'm CatKid!" I answer proudly. "I'm one whole-half cat and one whole-half kid. And my cat half has good hearing. That's how I heard you whispering."

18

"Plus, she's my best friend," Maddie says.

"Right-a-roonie!" I say.

"Oh," Kristie says. Then she smiles and I smile back. "Nice to meet you," she says.

"Nice to meet you right back," I say. But as soon as I finish saying it, I'm not so sure I mean it. That's because Kristie takes my spot next to Maddie on the story-time rug.

Preston is already sitting on the other side of Maddie. So there are zero sides for me to sit. I don't know where to turn my tail because I *always* sit next to Maddie!

I think Maddie should let Kristie know that. That's part of the showing-Kristie-around job. But Maddie doesn't say anything. She just lets Kristie sit there!

I make a little huff and sit down four spaces away from Maddie. That's called *sharing your best friend.*

But because of that sharing stuff, I have no one to whisper to during the story. Maddie is my number one whisper buddy, and she's too far away to hear me. Sometimes sharing is hard work.

I fold my arms and listen to the story. Only I don't giggle or go *oooohhhh* or *aaaahhhh* like I usually do. That's because story time isn't as much fun without Maddie to whisper to.

After the story, Mrs. Sparrow tells us that it's time for lunch. I'm still a little bit grumpy about the whole having-to-share-Maddie thing. But if there's one thing that makes me go all purry, it's lunch!

I race to the back of the room and grab my lunch box from my cubby. Then our class lines up to walk to the cafeteria. Maddie has to walk with Kristie because that's part of her job. I walk behind them. I can't even wait to get to our lunch table so we can all blabber.

Only know what?

Kristie takes my seat in the cafeteria, too, that's what!

She sits right down next to Maddie without even asking if it's okay. And it's *not* okay — I always sit next to Maddie.

I'm not so sure Kristie knows what

sharing means. So I march up to her and tap her on the shoulder.

"Um, that's my spot," I say.

Kristie looks up at me. "I'm sorry," she says.

Then Maddie looks up at me, too. "Would it be okay if Kristie sat here today?" she asks me.

I think about that for a second. Then I remember what Mrs. Sparrow said about making Kristie feel welcome. "Sure," I mumble, because I'm good at welcoming people.

"Thanks," Kristie says.

"You're welcome," I say. But I only half mean it.

I sit in the seat next to Kristie. I only make a teeny tiny grumble, because that's not so bad. Plus, I still want to know all about her old school.

So I ask her a gazillion questions.

"Were there any stinky boys, like Billy, in your class? Did your teacher give out special prizes like Mrs. Sparrow does? Did your principal have a shiny, bald head like our principal?"

When I finish asking all my questions, Kristie turns to look at me. But instead of answering them, her elbow knocks her chocolate milk right into my lap!

That makes me leap right out of my seat!

"Look, CatKid had an accident!" Billy shouts from across the cafeteria. Then the kids sitting around me go all giggly.

That giggling puts me in an extra grumpy mood.

"I'm sorry," Kristie says.

I don't say anything. I just make a frowny face because my whole entire lunch is ruined. I can't even wait for recess to start. There is no way recess can be ruined.

Only guess what?

Recess gets ruined, too, that's what!

That's because when I race out to the

monkey bars, Maddie is already at the top with Kristie.

And guess what else?

Maddie is teaching her our secret hand-clapping game, that's what else!

"Hey *Rat*Kid, it looks like the new girl is stealing your best friend!" Shelly teases.

I spin my tail around and see Shelly standing there with Olivia. Olivia is her best friend. She's in the other second-grade class, and she's just as snotty as Shelly.

"Yeah," Olivia says. "Without Maddie, you're just a stray cat!"

Even though my mom says I'm not supposed to hiss at anyone, I still feel like hissing at them!

"Shows what you know," I say. "It's part of Maddie's job to sit on the monkey bars with Kristie!" Then I stick out my tongue at them and walk away. That's what my dad calls *ignoring them*. Only it's not easy to ignore what Shelly and Olivia said, because every time I peek over at Maddie and Kristie, they're all giggly.

"Maybe Shelly's right," I mumble.

Maybe Kristie is trying to steal my best friend!

Chapter 4

Dad Knows Bestest

My dad is standing by the front door when I come home from school. He smiles real wide at me and waves.

I don't smile even a tiny bit back at him.

I toss my backpack on the floor and march over to the front window. It's my favorite spot in the whole house because it's the sunshiniest place. I keep a pillow there and some stuffed animals so that it's always ready in case I feel like catnapping.

But today, I don't even feel like napping. That's because I feel grumpy. And it's a cat fact that I can't nap when I'm grumpy.

"What's the matter, puppy?" my dad asks.

He always calls me puppy when I make sad eyes and droop my ears down. Most of the time that puppy name cracks my head up. But this time, it doesn't even make me the eensiest, weensiest bit giggly.

"Everything's the matter," I growl.

My dad comes over to my sunny spot and sits next to me. Then he scratches me behind the ears because that scratching behind the ears stuff usually cheers me up, but it doesn't today.

"Did you have a bad day?" my dad asks.

"The worst!" I tell him. "Worse than the time I lost my dollar at the park, and even worse than the time I scraped my knee on the playground."

"That sounds pretty bad," my dad says.

"Yeah," I mumble. "Only know what? It was all the new girl's fault, that's what!"

"There's a new girl in your class?" my dad asks.

I nod up and down and make a huff.

"Yepper," I say. "Her name's Kristie, but I think it should be Meanie!"

"That's not a nice thing to say," my dad tells me.

I cross my arms and make a double

huff. "That's because *she's* not nice!" I say. "Coming home on the school bus, she stole my seat next to Maddie and I had to sit next to Billy!" Then I hold my nose and wave my hand in front of my face to let my dad know how stinky sitting next to Billy is.

"Maybe she didn't know it was your seat," my dad says.

"Yes she did!" I say. Then I tell him everything that happened today, including the milk spilling and all the other seat-stealing stuff. "I added everything up and it equals Kristie being a friend stealer!"

"That sounds serious," my dad says.

"Mmm! Hmm!" I say. "It's super serious!"

"What did Maddie say?" my dad asks.

"She didn't say anything," I tell him. Then I explain to him about showing new students around. Moms and dads always need school stuff like that explained to them. "Mrs. Sparrow gave Maddie that job. So it was her job to be nice to Kristie today."

"That makes the picture a little clearer," my dad says.

I look around.

I don't see any picture.

"I didn't even draw a picture," I tell him.

"It's just an expression," he says, and I make a frown. My dad is always making up expressions that confuse my head. "Maybe Kristie is just trying to make friends, not steal them," my dad says.

"Really?" I ask.

"Sure," my dad says. "Think about how hard it would be for you to start a new school."

I rest my chin in my hands and think about a new school. A new school means a new teacher and new kids.

I wouldn't want a new teacher. Mrs. Sparrow is the nicest teacher in the whole second grade.

Plus, I wouldn't want to have to meet all new kids, either. A new school might be full of tail-tuggers like Billy.

"Yikes," I say. "A new school would be a *cat*-tastrophe!"

"See," my dad says. "Maybe you should give Kristie another chance."

And you know what?

My dad is one smart dad, that's what!

Then I promise to give Kristie another chance. "Just one, though," I say, and hold up one fin-ger to show my dad how many more chances Kristie is going to get.

Chapter 5

Last Chances

The next day, I, CatKid, try my bestest to be one nice kitty. I don't get mad when the school bus comes to pick me up and Kristie is sitting in my seat next to Maddie. I don't even make a growly noise!

Plus, I smile my whiskers and wave.

That's called *being the bigger cat*.

"Hi, CatKid," Maddie says.

"Hi, right back," I say. Then I sit my tail down in the seat behind them. And that's not so bad, because I can climb up on that seat and lean over. That way it's almost like I'm sitting there, too.

Only know what?

Mrs. Bus Driver sees me in the big mirror and tells me that I have to sit down, that's what!

"Yeah, those are the rules," Billy says from the seat next to mine.

I never promised to be nice to him, so I make a growl. "Yeah, well you're the biggest rule breaker on the whole entire bus, so there!" I holler at him.

I cross my arms and sit down.

I decide to count that as Kristie's

chance, because even if she didn't make up the bus rules, it's still almost her fault that I got in trouble.

But I decide to give Kristie another chance at morning recess. "Do you want to race with us?" I ask her.

Kristie wrinkles her nose and shakes her head. "I don't really like races," she says.

I, CatKid, cannot believe my cat ears!

"But *everybody* loves races," I say.

"Maybe we shouldn't race today," Maddie says.

I, CatKid, double don't believe my cat ears!

Then I don't believe my eyes, either, because Maddie takes two cookies out of her bag. She gives one to me and one to Kristie. Those cookies are supposed to be prizes! Plus, Maddie never gives anyone a cookie except for me!

If I didn't have a cookie to gobble up, I would be steamy mad!

And when Kristie takes my spot on the story-time rug for the second day in a row, I also feel steamy mad. But guess what? I don't even get grumpy, that's what!

That's because I have a secret plan.

My dad says I can invite Maddie over to my house after school for a playdate. And that playdate will be private. That means Kristie can't butt in.

I wait until recess before I ask. "Hey

Maddie," I say. "Do you want to come over to my house after school today?"

Maddie makes a frowny face.

That is one surprise frown! I wasn't even expecting it. That's because most of the time Maddie claps her hands and shouts, "Yippy Skippy Hooray!" whenever I invite her to my house.

"What's wrong?" I ask.

"Well, Kristie already invited me to her house," Maddie tells me. "And I already said yes."

This time I really do make a growly face. Then I stomp my paws and make a huff. Because ruining my playdate is what I, CatKid, call *the last straw*!

That means my dad was wrong and I was right. Kristie is absolutely, positively a friend stealer!

So that's it!

No more chances!

I, CatKid, am not letting her take my spot, or cookies, or friends ever again. From now on, I'm going to be one tough watch-cat!

Chapter 6

No More Miss Nice Cat!

The next morning at school, I'm busy thinking about how I'm going to guard my spots from Kristie when Mrs. Sparrow asks our class to pay attention.

"Today, we're going to work on a group project," Mrs. Sparrow tells us.

I forget all about that watch-cat stuff and clap my hands. Group projects are the best kinds of projects. They are almost as fun as cartoons, and I, CatKid, am what my dad calls *cartoon crazy*. Only that doesn't make much sense, because I'm not even crazy, that's why. Sometimes my dad is very silly for a dad.

"It's going to be a drawing project," Mrs. Sparrow says. "Each group is going to draw a picture of their neighborhood."

And guess what?

That cheers me up because drawing is my favorite subject, that's what! My tail goes all twitchy and I jump out of my seat. "I love to draw!" I holler out without raising my hand. Mrs. Sparrow calls that *being frisky*.

My class goes all giggly. That frisky stuff really cracks up their heads.

I cover my mouth real quick because hollering is against the rules. I wouldn't want to get in trouble during drawing time.

Lucky for me, I cover it fast enough that Mrs. Sparrow doesn't get mad.

Mrs. Sparrow tells us to think about different places in our neighborhood. I think about the ice-cream shop. It might be the most important place in my neighborhood. Plus, it makes me lick my whiskers.

"Now, I want you take out your markers and crayons and break into groups," Mrs. Sparrow says. "Each group will draw a picture of the different neighborhood places you came up with."

I smile real wide.

Paws down, that's the bestest project ever! I can't wait to start drawing the ice-cream shop. I'm going to draw ice cream all over the place!

I dig behind the books in my desk and grab my special marker collection. It's made up of all kinds of markers. Some of the tips are muddy because I like to mix colors, but it's still the best marker collection in the whole second grade.

"Got it," I say and pull the bag out of my desk. Then I remember about guarding my spot and I race over to Maddie before Kristie does.

"We're a group," I tell Maddie.

"You bet," Maddie says. "I wouldn't want to be in a group without you."

That makes me smile my whiskers. Only that smile disappears right away because Kristie comes over and asks to be part of our group too.

"We can all use my new marker set,"

Kristie says. "It has two hundred differ-ent colors!" Then she shows us that brand-new set.

I take a peek at it. None of the tips look muddy and not a single marker looks dried out. My special marker set doesn't look so special anymore.

"WOW!" Maddie says when she looks at those markers. "They're the best."

I make a frown.

Maddie used to think my markers were the best.

"Yeah, only know what?" I say to Kristie. "You can't join our group, so there."

Kristie and Maddie both stare at me.

"Why not?" Kristie asks.

"Because I was here first," I holler at her face.

"CatKid, you're not being very nice," Maddie says to me.

"Know why?" I say. "Because I'm not

even trying to be nice, that's why." I have been nice all week and Kristie hasn't been nice back. That means no more Miss Nice Cat!

Then I can't believe what happens next. Maddie takes Kristie's side! That's not even what best friends are supposed to do.

"I don't like it when you act mean," Maddie says.

"Yeah, well I don't like HER!" I say and point at that friend-stealer Kristie. "I don't want to be part of any group she's in," I say. Then I grab my markers and storm off. That's what my mom calls *putting my foot down*.

I go over and join Kendra and Preston's group. They might not be my bestest friends, but at least they still think my marker collection is special.

Only know what?

It doesn't even cheer me up, that's

what. Drawing the ice-cream shop isn't as much fun without Maddie. Preston and Kendra don't even giggle when I draw ice cream on people's heads in the picture.

"That doesn't look right," Kendra says.

"Yeah, you should start over," Preston says.

I take a deep breath and cross out the ice cream. I wish I could cross out this whole entire week instead.

Chapter 7

Best Friends for Never

At recess the next day, I take my three favorite stuffed animals out of my backpack and sit them down with me. Those stuffed animals are what I call my *Feel*

Better Gang. I brought them with me to school so that I wouldn't have to play with that friend-stealer Kristie.

Mr. Raccoon Bear sits on my lap because he is my oldest stuffed animal. I got him when I was still a kittenkid. I think maybe he's even older than me!

Next to him is Hoppy Hop Hop, my stuffed bunny, and Tigerlina, my stuffed tiger. Those two are good stuffed animals. When I grow up, I want to be able to hop like a bunny and roar like a tiger.

"Guess what?" I say to all three of them. "You guys are now my bestest friends, that's what."

That makes them all smiley. But they are always smiley, so I'm not sure they really understand. So I make them each nod their heads. That way I know they under-stand.

I tell them all about the ice-cream

47

shop I drew. "I even drew ice cream on everybody's head," I say. Then I cover my mouth and giggle so that they know that ice cream on the head is funny stuff.

Next, I try to teach them the hand-clapping game that Maddie and I used to play way back when we were best friends. I show Mr. Raccoon Bear first, but he doesn't even clap back. Neither does Tigerlina or Hoppy Hop Hop.

I scratch my head and sigh at them. "I'm not sure you guys know the rules of best friends," I say. So I explain the rules to them.

It's no use though.

They just keep staring at me with smiley faces.

Just then, I hear someone standing behind me.

My mouth drops open and I spin my tail around. It's Mrs. Sparrow! I didn't even know she was watching me. Some-times she is one really sneaky teacher.

"Is something bothering you?" Mrs. Sparrow asks.

I shake my head back and forth.

"Why aren't you playing with Maddie today?"

"Because we're not even best friends anymore," I tell her. "Now that Kristie and her are new friends, there's no room for me." Then I grab my Feel Better

Gang and give them a big hug, but even that doesn't stop me from making sad eyes.

Then Mrs. Sparrow sits down next to me and scratches me behind my ears. Most of the time that makes me go all purry. But this time it only makes me a teeny tiny bit purry.

"So that's why you're playing with your stuffed animals?" she asks. That's because she is one smart lady. She always knows things without anyone telling her first. Sometimes I think maybe she knows everything in the whole world.

I nod my head up and down.

"CatKid, sometimes best friends need to make new friends," she says.

My eyes open real wide. I've never heard that before, and I wonder if it's really one of the rules of best friends.

"Really?" I ask. "But why would Maddie want another friend if she has a *purr*-fect friend like me?"

"Some people like to have a lot of friends," Mrs. Sparrow says. She says maybe I could make new friends, too. "And just because you have new friends, it doesn't mean you and Maddie can't still be *best* friends."

I'm not so sure. Maybe the rules for grown-up friends work differently than the rules for second-grade friends.

"Okay, I'll try," I mumble.

I sure hope she's right about making new friends. Because I, CatKid, don't like being a stray cat.

Chapter 8

New Best Friends

I climb aboard the school bus when it comes to my house the next morning. "Hi, Mrs. Bus Driver," I say, only I don't wave. That's because I'm being extra careful not to wrinkle the paper in my hands.

It's a drawing of my pet goldfish with ice cream on its head. I made it for my new best friend. I just have to find a new best friend first.

I take a look at all the kids and try to pick one. The first kid I see is a boy. I, CatKid, will NOT be best friends with a boy. The next kid I see is a kindergart-ner, and I don't want to be friends with one of them. That's because sometimes they cry.

Then I see Lauren. She's a girl and she's in my class. Plus she is sitting by herself. That makes her a *purr*-fect choice! So I sit my tail down right next to her.

"Hi, CatKid," Lauren says.

"Hi, right back," I say.

That's called making new best friends.

So I give the drawing to Lauren. That drawing cracks Lauren's head up! Her laughing makes me smile real happy.

"Thanks," she says.

"You're welcome," I say.

When the bus pulls up to our school, I grab Lauren's hand. "Let's race to the monkey bars," I say to her.

"Okay," she says.

Then I race as fast as I can. I get to the monkey bars first and leap to the top. "I win," I shout when Lauren gets there. Then I hold out my hand.

Lauren looks at my hand. She gives me zero cookies.

"The winner is supposed to get a cookie," I tell her. "Those are the rules."

"Oh," Lauren says. "I don't have any

cookies. I'm not allowed to eat sugar."
Then she opens her lunchbox and
hands me a carrot stick. "You can
have this."

I look at the carrot and stick out my
tongue because carrots are stinky. "That's
okay," I say. Then I give it back to her.

I ask Lauren what she wants to play.

Lauren scratches her head. "I know,"
she says. "Let's play spelling bee. We'll
each take turns spelling words."

I make a grumpy face.

"Only know what?" I tell her. "I don't
like spelling, that's what. How about we
play a hand-clapping game instead?"

"Okay," Lauren says. Then I show her
the Miss Special Cat clapping game. Only
Lauren doesn't like that chant. She says
it's not the right words.

"Yeah, I know," I say. "I made them up.
That's called using my imagination."

"But I don't know the made up words," Lauren says.

"That's okay, I'll teach you," I say.

Only Lauren's not really good at learning the new words. She keeps messing up. So finally I agree to say the right words even though I don't like saying them. But that's what new best friends do. It's my job to teach Lauren all about being new best friends.

And Lauren sure has a lot to learn!

At story time, I teach her about whispering. "That's a good part," I whisper to her when a good part in the story happens. But every time I whisper to her, she makes a *ssshhhh* sound.

"But we're whisper buddies," I explain to her.

"I don't like to whisper during stories," she whispers back.

I, CatKid, can't even believe my ears

because whispering is the second-most fun part about story time.

I take a deep breath and shrug my shoulders.

I never had to teach Maddie any of the rules before. I didn't know making new friends was such hard work.

Chapter 9

Almost Friends

Today is a special day. That's because today is the day our class has library time. We all get to go down to the library and Mrs. Morris, the librarian, helps each of us pick out a book to read.

When Mrs. Sparrow tells us to line up in pairs, I don't even try to be Maddie's partner. I walk right over to Lauren and ask her to be my partner.

Then I look over my shoulder to make sure Maddie saw me.

Only know what?

Maddie isn't even looking at me, that's what! She's already Kristie's partner.

I turn around and make a huff.

I'll show Maddie that me and Lauren are better best friends than her and Kristie!

So when we get to the library, I ask Lauren what kind of book she's going to pick.

"I don't know," Lauren says.

"We should pick the same kind of book," I tell her. "Then we can be reading buddies."

Once upon a time, me and Maddie used to do that. One week we'd pick a unicorn story and then the next week we'd both read a cat story.

"Okay," Lauren says.

"Super-duper!" I say.

Mrs. Morris comes over to us when it's our turn to be helped. "What kind of book can I help you girls find?" she asks.

"I know! I know!" I whisper-shout. "We want to read a book about cats. Especially one about cats that chase mice." Then I lean over and whisper in Lauren's ear that those are the best kinds of books.

"Those sound like babyish books," Lauren says.

My eyes open really wide!

There is nothing babyish about chasing mice!

"How about we read a mystery book?" Lauren asks.

I, CatKid, don't like mystery books. They confuse my head. But then I see Maddie and Kristie and they both have

books about unicorns. I'm not going to let them be better best friends than me and Lauren, so I nod my head okay.

When we get back to our classroom, Mrs. Sparrow tells us to put our library books in our cubbies. I march over and shove that mystery book all the way in the back.

But then guess what?

I see a shiny red envelope in my cubby, too, that's what! Plus, it has my name spelled on it.

I open up that envelope right away.

And guess what else? I can't believe my eyes, that's what else! That's because it's an invitation to Kristie's birthday party.

"I got an invitation? Yippity do da!" I shout.

"Everyone in the whole class got one, Dumb Ears!" Shelly says. But I'm so happy that I don't even care about that Dumb Ears stuff. That's because I'm what my mom calls *a party animal*.

I'm so excited that I forget to stop at Lauren's desk and run right over to Maddie's desk instead. I don't even pretend to be mad at her anymore. Then I give her the thumbs up because she loves parties as much as I do.

"Look," I tell her. "It says there will be lots of games!"

"Yeah, and pony rides," Maddie says and points to the bottom of the invitation.

I take another look at the invitation. "I didn't even see that. I LOVE, LOVE, LOVE ponies!" I shout. Me and Maddie have always wanted to be cowgirls. Now we can pretend for real!

I'm so happy I start to go all purry.

Maddie covers her mouth and giggles.

Then Kristie comes over and I'm not even mad at her, either. "Thanks for the invitation," I say to her. She smiles and says that I'm welcome.

Only know what?

Then she ruins everything, that's what!

"Maddie, will you be my teammate for the games at my party?" Kristie asks.

I make a GULP!

Me and Maddie are always a team. We're the bestest team ever! She can't be on Kristie's team *and* my team.

I look at Maddie but Maddie doesn't look back.

"Sure, that'll be fun," Maddie tells Kristie.

I can't believe my cat ears!

I stomp my foot down and make a double huff. Then I march over to Lauren's desk and ask her to be my teammate at the party.

"Of course!" Lauren says. "You're the best at games."

I smile at her. From now on, me and Lauren are best friends. And this time, I mean it!

Chapter 10

Party Plan

I race out of my bedroom and stand at the top of the stairs. Then I yell at the top of my lungs.

"MOM!" I scream. "COME QUICK!" I howl.

There's a rule in my house about screaming and howling. The rule is that I'm not supposed to do those things.

My mom reminds me of that rule when she comes up the stairs. She covers her ears and says, "Please don't shout."

"Okay, but this is an emergency!" I tell her. I'm allowed to shout during an emergency. That's because once upon a time when I was really little, I had a bathroom emergency and I didn't shout. It was a messy emergency. That's when my mom and dad changed the screaming rule.

"What is it?" my mom asks.

"I looked everywhere and I can't find my new dress for the party," I say. My mom bought me a pretty red dress for Kristie's party. It's *cat*-tastic! It even has white flowers on it. But when I went to my room to get ready, it was lost.

I took everything out of my closet.

I took everything out of my dresser.

I even took everything out from under my bed.

"It's nowhere!" I tell my mom.

My mom steps into my bedroom and her eyes go all big. "What happened in here? It looks like a wild animal got loose," she says when she sees the mess in my room.

"Yeah, only know what? I'm only one whole-half a wild animal," I tell her. Then I laugh because that wild animal stuff makes me giggly.

My mom doesn't think it's giggly though. She puts her hands on her hips and takes a deep breath. That's what she does whenever she thinks I'm being a silly kitty.

"Your dress is in my room. I put it there so it wouldn't get wrinkled," my mom says.

"Oh," I say. Then I look at all the stuff

I tossed around my room. "That was good thinking," I tell my mom.

Then I race into my mom and dad's room and find my dress. I put it right on and look in the mirror. It matches my tail *purr*-fectly!

I can't wait to get to the party and show my dress to Lauren. That's because me and Lauren are best friends, and we're going to have the best time. Plus, we're going to win all the prizes.

"Well, hello, Miss Fancy Pants," my dad says when he sees me in my dress.

I scratch my head.

Then I look down at my knees.

"Only, I'm not even wearing pants," I tell my dad. "I checked. No pants. Just underpants."

My dad smiles. He always smiles when he says the wrong things. I don't know why. When I say the wrong answers in school, I make a frown.

"You ready to go?" he asks.

"Yepper." I nod.

But then I remember something that I forgot. I hold up my finger in the air. "One second," I say. Then I run back up to my bedroom. Kristie's present is sitting on my desk.

I grab the present and hurry down the stairs.

Then I grab my dad and pull him to the door.

I can't even wait to show Maddie that me and Lauren are the best bestest friends in the whole wide world! Plus, I really, really, really want to ride on one of those ponies.

Chapter 11

Party Animal

I, CatKid, wave good-bye to my dad when he drops me off at the party. "'Bye!" I holler. Then I race my tail up to Kristie's house and ring the doorbell.

Kristie's mom answers the door. "You must be CatKid," she says.

I make a surprised face.

Moms are super-good guessers. I don't even know how she knew my name!

"Right-a-roonie!" I tell her. Then I smile. That's what I call being one cool cat.

Kristie's mom says the rest of the

kids are in the other room. She lets me in and points the way. I hurry inside and see a whole bunch of kids from my class.

I see Kendra and Preston eating chips. I wave at them and they wave back.

Then I see Billy and Bradley. They are playing a card game, plus, Billy and Bradley are stinky to me. So I don't even wave at them.

Next I see Maddie. I almost wave, but she doesn't see me. She's too busy whispering to Kristie. So I keep my wave to myself. Besides, I have a new best friend to wave to.

I spin my tail around until I see Lauren. She is standing by the potato chips. That is one good place to stand because potato chips are what I call YUMMY!

"Hi, CatKid!" she says. "I like your dress."

"Thanks! I picked it out all by myself,"
I tell her. Then I grab a handful of potato
chips and gobble them all up.

"This is going to be a fun party," Lauren
says to me.

"You betcha!" I tell her. "First we're
going to win all the prizes, then
we're going to gallop on those ponies,
and *then* we get to eat cake!"

Then I grab Lauren's hand and walk

over to Preston and Kendra. I tell them both how me and Lauren are a team.

"Don't you think we're a better team than Maddie and Kristie?" I ask.

Preston shrugs his shoulders.

So does Kendra.

I make a big breath. "Well, we are," I tell them. "And we'll prove it!"

Just then, Kristie's mom tells us all that it's time for the first game. "We're going to have a three-legged race," she says.

I clap my hands. "Goody gumdrops with fish on top!" I say to Lauren.

Lauren giggles at the *fish on top* thingy. That makes me smile because I think she's finally learning the rules of best friends.

The whole entire party moves to the backyard. It is one big backyard, too! I bet my whole front yard and backyard added together would fit in it. And

another thing, there are balloons all over the place! They are taped to all the chairs and even to the fence.

But my favorite part about Kristie's yard is the pick-up truck parked all the way in the back. That's because there's a trailer attached to it, and I, CatKid, know for a fact that there is a real live pony in that trailer!

If it weren't for the race, I would go right over there and pet that pony. But first things first! I can't even wait to show everybody that me and Lauren are the best team ever.

So we go over to the starting spot and wait for the game to begin.

"*Pssst!* Guess what?" I tell Lauren. "It's a cat fact that three-legged races are my best kind of race. That means we'll win for sure."

Chapter 12

Not All Fun and Games

My plan doesn't work one bit. Me and Lauren don't win the three-legged race. We don't even come in second or third or even fourth.

We come in last place because Lauren keeps tripping over my tail.

Next is the wheelbarrow race. That race doesn't go any better. I push too fast and Lauren is too slow at being the wheel. So I keep tumbling over her and we keep ending up on the ground.

Then we come in last for the egg-on-a-spoon race, too. Lauren kept dropping

the egg. By the time the race was over, our egg was only a bunch of gooey gunk!

"I'm not very good at races," Lauren tells me after the team games are over. Only I don't need her to tell me that. I already figured it out all by myself.

I make a frown.

"That's okay," I say. That's called being a good friend.

At least Maddie and Kristie didn't win. That's because Kristie isn't very good at races either. But it stills ruffles my whiskers because Shelly and Olivia won one race. And Billy and Bradley won two.

Those two teams are what I call *yucky teams.* Plus, they are sore winners. They don't stop bragging about it.

"We won and you lost," Billy teases. Then he shows me the toy frog he won as a special prize. I make a growl. It sure is one fancy frog toy.

"No one likes a show-off," I tell him. But I have a secret. My secret is that if I won that frog, I'd show it off all over the place, too.

Next, Kristie's mom tells us that it's time to go inside. "We're going to play musical chairs," she says.

I, CatKid, jump up and down. That's because musical chairs is a fun game. Also, it's not a team game. That means I might win. Because even though I like Lauren, I like special prizes, too.

All of us kids form a circle around the chairs. By accident, I stand next to Maddie.

"Good luck," Maddie says to me.

I'm supposed to say good luck right back, but I keep my mouth zippered shut. That's because I'm still not talking to her.

All of the sudden, the room fills with music!

I put my ears back. My ears always go back when a surprise sound sneaks up on me. My tail even goes bushy, too!

Someone taps me on the back.

I spin around and see Billy standing there.

"Hey tail face, you're supposed to start walking," he says.

I make a small hiss at him. "Yeah, I knew that," I say. Then I start walking around the chairs with everyone else. When the music stops, I leap onto one of them and sit my tail down.

I look around.

Billy is still standing.

"Hey stinky face, you're supposed to sit down," I say with a giggle. That's called getting even.

One by one, there are less kids walking around the chairs. And before I know it, there are only two kids left. One of them is me, CatKid. The other one makes me go GULP!

That's because it's Maddie.

This is my chance to show her that I'm the best. So when Mrs. Kristie's Mom starts the music, I dance around the last chair very carefully.

But guess what?

When the music stops, I'm on the wrong side of the chair.

But then guess what else?

Maddie doesn't even sit in the chair! So I sit down first. That means I win!

I start to clap my hands and cheer. Then everyone else starts cheering, too, even Maddie! But you know what? For some reason when I see Maddie cheering, I don't feel like cheering anymore.

Chapter 13

Specialest Prize of All

I, CatKid, get my special prize after the game is over. It's a stuffed giraffe named Raffy. I came up with that name all by myself. It's my new favorite stuffed animal. I think my other stuffed animals will really like him.

But Raffy makes me only a teeny tiny bit happy. That's because he really belongs to Maddie. She should have won musical chairs.

I walk over to Maddie and hold out Raffy. "Here," I say. "He's yours, fair and square."

Maddie giggles. "Silly kitty, you won!"
she says. "He's yours!"

"But you let me win," I say.

Maddie smiles. "That's because I
know how much you like special prizes.
So I wanted you to have it. That's what
best friends do."

I, CatKid, can't even believe my ears.

"But isn't Kristie your best friend?"
I ask.

"Kristie is my friend, but you'll always be my bestest friend," Maddie says.

"Then how come you let her do all of our best-friend stuff?" I ask. "You kept letting her take my spot next to you. You played our secret hand-clapping game with her. You had a playdate with her instead of me. You were on her team instead of mine. Also, you told her you liked her markers. That's five things!"

I counted them on my fingers. Then I show my whole entire hand to Maddie so she can see those five things.

Maddie lowers her eyes and folds her hands together. I call that her sorry face. She always makes that face when she's feeling sorry.

"I didn't mean to leave you out all those times," she says. "I just wanted Kristie to feel welcome."

"Really?" I ask.

"Really," Maddie says.

I smile my whiskers. Then I grab my tail and spin around on one leg to do my happy dance. "Yippy!" I shout, because I, CatKid, am happy to have my best friend back.

But then I stop still and my eyes go all wide.

"What's wrong?" Maddie asks.

"I forgot that Lauren is my new best friend," I say. I don't even want to make Lauren sad. She's an A-plus friend.

Maddie covers her mouth and giggles. I don't see anything giggly about it. But then Maddie points over to the snack table. "I think Lauren already has a new best friend," she says.

I spin my tail around and see Lauren

standing next to Kristie. They're all gig-gly and whispery. And this time, I don't even mind Kristie being a friend-stealer, because she and Lauren are what I call a good team.

Then Maddie takes my hand and hur-ries me over to her backpack. "I brought us a surprise," she tells me.

My tail goes waggy.

Maddie always has the best surprises!

She reaches into her backpack and takes out two cowgirl bandannas. "These are for the pony rides," she says. "We can pretend we're cowgirls!"

I leap right into the air and land on my feet. "It's what we've always wanted to be our whole entire lives!"

I give Maddie a great big, GINOR-MOUS hug!

"You're the best friend a cat ever had," I tell her. It's the truth, too! Maddie always knows exactly what I like! No one

in the whole world is better at being my friend than Maddie.

Then I tell her that I'm sorry, too. "It's okay with me if Kristie sits next to you sometimes," I say. Then I hold up my finger and add, "Only not during the pony rides, okay?"

"Deal!" Maddie says.

Then we race outside and over to the trailer and get ready to saddle up! And

guess what? There are two real live ponies. That means we get to ride them at the same time.

We both yell "Yee-Haa" the whole time we're riding on the ponies. We have so much fun that I don't ever want it to end. It's the best party ever!

When it's time to go home, my dad comes to pick me up. I run right over to his car with my new giraffe and climb in.

"Did you have a good time, Kitten?" he asks.

I'm so happy that I don't even make a frown when he calls me that kitten name. "Mmm! Hmm!" I tell him and nod my head up and down. "And you know what?"

"What?" my dad asks.

"You were right, that's what!" I tell him. "Even if me and Maddie make new friends, we will always be bestest friends!"

A Little Sister Can Be A Big Pain— Especially If She Has Magical Powers!

Can it be true? Adorable, annoying five-year-old Violet actually has magical powers? For eight-year-old Mabel, being a big sister will never be the same.

Mabel knows being a big sister has a power all its own. But when Violet conjures up a pool, Mabel doesn't know how she will explain it to the neighbors—or her parents!

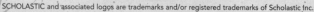